Troy's Cold

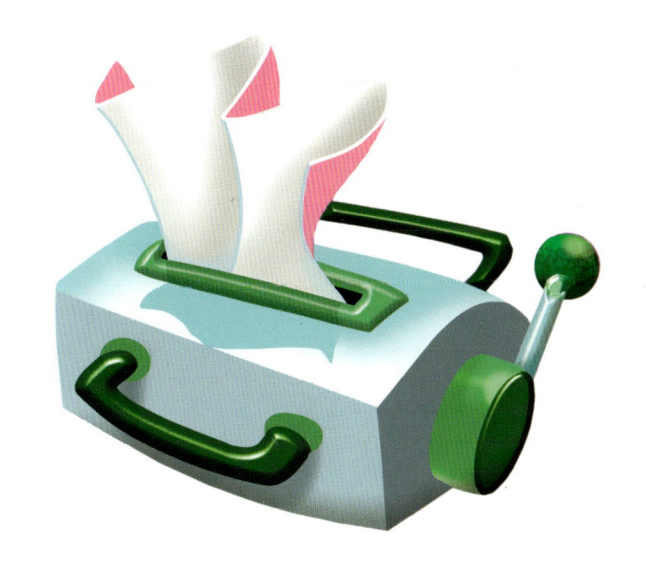

Written by Joy Cowley
Illustrated by Gaston Vanzet

It was raining outside, and
Troy was sick in bed.
His eyes were red,
and so was his nose.
He sneezed and sneezed.
Aa-choo! Aa-choo!

3

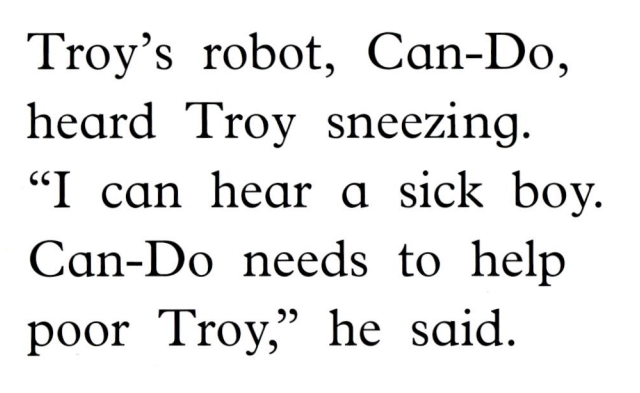

Troy's robot, Can-Do, heard Troy sneezing. "I can hear a sick boy. Can-Do needs to help poor Troy," he said.

"Me, too!" buzzed Me2 the computer.

"I'm all right," said Troy, in a croaky voice. "I just need to rest."

But Can-Do and Me2 really wanted to help Troy get better.

"Maybe he needs new software," buzzed Me2.

"No, I think he has a rusty throat," said Can-Do.
He picked up an oil can.

"Open wide," said Can-Do.

"No, no, no!" said Troy. "I'm not rusty. I've got a virus!"

"A virus?" buzzed Me2. "Oh no! Troy might lose his memory!"

"We need to get him a new hard drive," said Can-Do.

They raced to the store.

"A new hard drive for Troy, please," buzzed Me2.

"I don't know the Troy computer," said the store owner.
"What model is it?"

"Troy is a *boy* model," said Can-Do.

"Boys don't have hard drives," the store owner replied.

Me2 and Can-Do walked home in the rain.
They were sad and wet.

"I think I'm getting a rusty throat," said Can-Do.

Troy was waiting for them.
He was feeling a lot better.

"Why did you go out in the rain?" he asked.

"We wanted to help you," said Can-Do, in a croaky voice.

"We wanted to get you a new hard drive," buzzed Me2.

Troy laughed. He dried Can-Do and Me2, and he gave Can-Do some oil.
"Open wide," he said.

Then he read them a story. It was about a helpful robot and a helpful computer.

"That's me," said Can-Do sleepily.

"Me, too," said Me2.